by Jane B. Mason

BATTLE BUGS
OF
OUTER SPACE

illustrated by
Art Baltazar

raintree

a Capstone company — publishers for children

Starring...

BZZD
THE GREEN LANTERN

GREEN LANTERN
BUG CORPS

SINESTRO BUG CORPS

CONTENTS

Meet the Corps **4**

Chapter 1
PEST CRIME **6**

Chapter 2
IT'S A HIT! **18**

Chapter 3
BUG BATTLE **32**

KNOW YOUR SUPER-PETS..........................**50**
JOKES...**52**
GLOSSARY **53**
MEET THE AUTHOR AND ILLUSTRATOR.....**54**

SUPER-PET HERO FILE 011:
GREEN LANTERN BUG CORPS

Bio: With their superpowered rings, the Green Lantern Bug Corps guards the universe and protects it from evil.

Gratch
Species: mantis

Bzzd
Species: space bug

Eeny
Species: ant

Zhoomp
Species: grasshopper

Buzzoo
Species: bee

Fossfur
Species: firefly

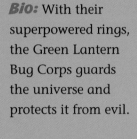

Super hero pal:
JOHN STEWART
*Green Lantern,
Space Sector 2814*

SUPER-PET ENEMY FILE 011:
SINESTRO BUG CORPS

Eezix
Species: mosquito

Tootz
Species: stink bug

Bio: The creepy crawly critters of the Sinestro Bug Corps use their yellow rings to spread fear across the universe.

Donald
Species: cockroach

Webbik
Species: tarantula

Waxxee
Species: earwig

Fimble
Species: stick insect

Super-villain pal:
SINESTRO
Leader of Sinestro Corps Base: Qward

PEST CRIME

CRAAAACK!

The baseball soared into left field at Coast City Stadium. The batter dropped his bat and ran to first base.

"**Yay!**" Bzzd shouted. "**Go, go, go!**" His wings flapped wildly. He watched number 38 approach second base.

Bzzd loved baseball. He was having a great time here on Earth. The Sun was shining. The fans were cheering. And the Rockets, his favourite team, were winning!

Bzzd was not your average baseball fan. He was not even human! He was an insect. He was also a member of the **Green Lantern Corps.**

Using powerful rings, the Green Lanterns protected the universe from evil-doers. This giant-sized job rarely left Bzzd time to relax.

"Go, go, go!" Bzzd shouted again. He zoomed behind the pitcher for a better view of the action.

The next Rockets player was up to bat. The pitcher from the other team, the Warriors, looked cross. Who could blame him? His team was losing 6–2 in the bottom of the seventh inning. Time was running out.

The batter stepped up to the plate.

Strike one! Strike two! Then the pitcher

hurled another fast ball, and the batter

swung for a third time.

"A cockroach!" someone suddenly

screamed in the stands.

"It's a hit!" the announcer shouted.

Bzzd wanted to watch the play. But as a **Green Lantern**, he knew that duty called. He soared into the stands to check out the screams.

WHOOSH!

"Help me! Help me!" a woman yelled at the top of her lungs.

Bzzd hovered over the woman's shoulder. Sure enough, a giant cockroach was crawling all over her jumbo hot dog. Not just any cockroach, either. It was **Donald!**

Bzzd and Donald had crossed paths before. Donald was a member of the evil **Sinestro Bug Corps**. He liked to stir up trouble. The cockroach smiled and took a bite out of the lady's hot dog.

Bzzd scowled.

Hot dogs were a big part of baseball. Fans were supposed to be able to enjoy them at games.

Donald rubbed his legs together greedily. He took another bite.

FWOOOOSH!

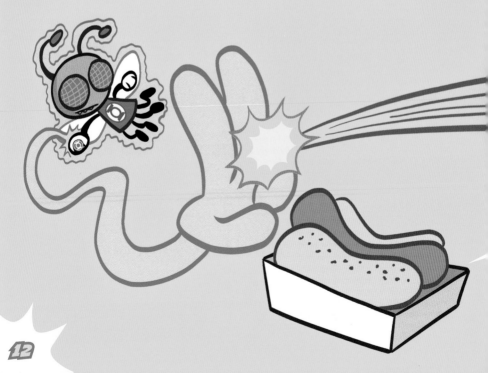

Bzzd's power ring flashed, shooting a ray of green energy. He imagined a finger flicking Donald off the hot dog.

 Half a second later, Donald was squirming on his back on the stadium floor.

"Hey!" shouted the cockroach.

BWEEOOM!

Yellow light shot out of Donald's ring, knocking Bzzd off balance. Donald tackled Bzzd in mid-air, and the two fell to the ground in a heap.

"If you want a hot dog, get your own," Bzzd said calmly. He wriggled himself free and took a step back.

"Mind your business!" said Donald.

"Yeah, mind your own business," said a second voice.

Bzzd spotted **Webbik**, a Sinestro

spider, staring at him from an empty

seat. Webbik was a tarantula with

a tiny brain and a knack for trouble.

"You're no match for us, you winged

weakling!" Webbik snorted.

"Warriors rule!" Donald added.

Bzzd knew he should ignore their insults. He also knew he had to stand up to the bug bullies!

"Is that why the Warriors are eating the Rockets' dust?" Bzzd replied.

Bzzd saw a flash of anger in the eyes of the evil bugs. A second later, their rings began firing in all directions. If these villains were not stopped, this innocent pastime would soon become the world's worst pest crime!

Chapter 2

IT'S A HIT!

Bzzd was no scaredy-bug, but he

was no fool, either. He took off as fast

as his vibrating wings could carry him.

 The sound of

his beating wings hummed in his ears.

He rounded third base and approached

the pitcher's mound.

Donald and Webbik were behind him. Their yellow rings continued to blast rays of light. **BWEEOOM!**

Meanwhile, the game was in the top of the eighth inning. The Warriors were up to bat. The first pitch sailed across the plate. The batter swung.

"Strike one!" yelled the umpire.

Bzzd darted over to the Rockets' dugout. A beam of yellow light behind him got closer and closer.

"Zap him!" Donald shouted.

A wild yellow light shot out of Webbik's ring and blasted Bzzd. The Green Lantern felt dizzy. **He could not fly straight!**

Up ahead, a row of Warriors sat on the bench, waiting for their turn to bat. Player number 43 took off his baseball cap to scratch his head. Bzzd tried to steer clear, but the whole world was yellow and spinning!

 He buzzed frantically.

Oof! Too late. Bzzd had already landed

in a giant head of curly hair.

"Ah! Get it out! Get it out!" shouted

player number 43. "There's something

in my hair!"

Webbik and Donald roared with laughter as number 43 swiped at his head. He nearly squashed Bzzd flat.

Bzzd focused on his ring. He shot out an arc of green energy. Then he soared out of the sweaty tangles like a jet.

Bzzd glanced over his shoulder. The Sinestro Corps duo crashed into a giant pole at the edge of the dugout. They fell to the dirt floor in a tangle of spider and cockroach legs.

Bzzd smirked and headed over to the home plate. The baseball game was still in the eighth inning. The score was still 6–2. The Warriors had two outs, and the batter had two strikes.

"Looks like it's do or die for your team!" said Bzzd.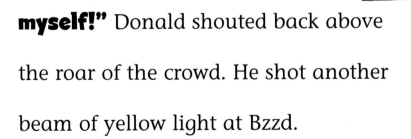

"I couldn't have said it better myself!" Donald shouted back above the roar of the crowd. He shot another beam of yellow light at Bzzd.

The pitcher wound up. The ball sailed towards home plate. Bzzd heard it coming and tried to dodge, but the yellow light held him back. Donald and Webbik crashed into him, and the ball smashed into all three bugs.

The Warriors' batter struck the ball hard, sending it flying.

"Whoooaaa!" the threesome cried. The baseball – and the bugs – sailed over the stands and out of the park.

WHAM!!!

The bugs landed in a stinky skip behind the playing field.

"Where are we?" Bzzd asked.

"In heaven!" Donald cried out.

Bzzd looked around. **"Heaven?"** he repeated.

"Yes, heaven," Donald confirmed. "A giant pile of rubbish!"

Bzzd wiggled his antennae in the air. It did smell pretty good.

"Lunchtime!" Donald cried. He crawled over to a half-eaten pastry covered with gooey slime.

"I'm a little hungry myself," Webbik said, sniffing some mouldy peanuts.

Bzzd started to bite into an old hot dog. **FZZZZZZT!**

A beam of energy suddenly struck him in the back. "Ouch!" he yelled.

"Back off, mangy maggot!" shouted Donald. He pointed his power ring at Bzzd. "This rubbish is ours!"

"Yeah!" Webbik agreed. "And don't try anything funny. **We've got you outnumbered!"**

WHOOSH! Just then, a neon light flashed through the skip.

The Green Lantern firefly, **Fossfur**,
suddenly landed next to Bzzd. "Beep!
Wrong," he said, blinking his tail on
and off. "I believe the score is tied."

"Ha! Think again!" shouted Donald.

The skip started shaking like an

earthquake. It rocked from side to side

and up and down. Then, from beneath

the piles of rotten rubbish, **other**

Sinestro Corps Bugs appeared.

Each one carried its own yellow ring.

"It's game over for you two," said Donald. The cockroach pointed his power ring at the Green Lanterns. The other evil insects followed his lead.

"Beep! Wrong again," Fossfur said. "This bug battle has just begun!"

BUG BATTLE

Bzzd and Fossfur held their power rings into the air. Together, they repeated the Green Lantern oath:

"In brightest day, in blackest night, no evil shall escape my sight. Let those who worship evil's might, beware my power – Green Lantern's light!"

Bzzd and Fossfur each imagined a giant bottle of insect spray. A second later, the objects appeared from their rings. The Green Lanterns pointed the bottles at the bad news bugs and blasted them with a mist of energy.

The Sinestro Corps Bugs started coughing and falling down.

"Phew!" said Donald the cockroach, trying to fan away the mist with his tiny legs. "That's a rotten thing to do!"

"Did someone say rotten?" asked **Tootz**, another Sinestro Bug, from near by. "They don't call me a stink bug for nothing!" The smelly bug let out an awful odour of his own.

Bzzd and Fossfur could not handle the stench. They created a stink-proof bubble with their rings and hid inside.

The Sinestro Corps Bugs surrounded them. "Looks like you're caught in a pickle," said Donald the cockroach. "Are you ready to give up?"

Fossfur the firefly blinked his behind on and off. On and off. On and off.

"Is he surrendering?" Donald asked the evil mosquito next to him.

"Don't ask me!" said Eezix. "I don't speak glow bug."

"He's not giving up," shouted Bzzd. "He's calling for reinforcements!"

Suddenly, four more Green Lantern insects dived into the skip. They shot glowing green baseballs at Donald and the other Sinestro Bugs.

"Bet you didn't see that curveball coming," joked Bzzd with a laugh.

"Ah!" cried Donald. He dodged from side to side, trying to avoid the wild pitches. "What should we do?"

"Branch out!" shouted **Fimble** the stick insect. **"They can't hit us all!"**

The Sinestro Corps Bugs scattered in all directions, and the Green Lanterns gave chase. **Fossfur** took off after **Tootz**. **Gratch** the mantis tracked down **Webbik**. **Buzzoo** the bee zoomed towards **Eezix** the mosquito.

Bzzd set his sights on **Donald**.

KA-POW! KA-POW!

He fired two glowing green stingers

at the cockroach. He missed.

"Haha!" Donald exclaimed. "That's

two strikes. One more, and you're out!"

He held out his ring and returned fire.

On the far side of the skip, **Eeny** the ant faced off against the Sinestro stick insect. Fimble was more than twice the Green Lantern's size.

"Ha! It's not even fair," said Fimble, laughing at the teensy ant. "I'll snap this puny pest like a twig!"

"Let's see if YOU like being picked on," shouted Eeny. **"Or should I say pecked on?"** The ant created a giant woodpecker with his ring. It chased after the stick insect like a tasty treat.

Meanwhile, the other insect enemies

shot beams of green and yellow light

back and forth at each other.

BEEOOM! BEEOOM!

The smelly skip quickly turned into

a scene of bug rage.

"Give up!" said Donald. "You're no match for our pest powers!"

Fossfur started blinking again.

"Now what?" asked Donald.

The firefly pointed to the sky. His tail blinked faster and faster.

"Listen," said Waxee the earwig. "I think I hear something." The Green Lantern bug looked up, and the other pests followed his gaze.

A giant baseball fell from the sky like a two-tonne bomb. The insects flew in all directions, nearly squashed by the massive ball.

"Who did that?" said Donald.

Lying on the floor, Bzzd suddenly remembered the baseball game. He flew to the top of the skip and looked out. The stadium scoreboard read 6–6 in the bottom of the ninth inning. The Warriors had just drawn the game with a mighty grand slam.

"Ha!" Donald exclaimed. He and

the other bugs had crawled up beside

Bzzd. "Looks like this game isn't over."

"Neither is this bug battle," said

Bzzd. **"But for now, how about we

call it a draw?"**

The other bugs agreed.

"Besides," added Bzzd, "you know

what extra innings mean, don't you?"

The bugs looked out at the stadium.

Thousands of hungry fans munched

on hot dogs, popcorn, and peanuts.

Fossfur blinked his tail. Tootz the
stink bug let out a giant burp. Webbik
the tarantula licked his hairy lips.

"Extra rubbish!" Donald exclaimed.

"**Exactly**," said Bzzd, leading them
towards the stands. **"Play ball!"**

END

KNOW YOUR HERO PETS

1. Krypto
2. Streaky
3. Beppo
4. Comet
5. Ace
6. Robin Robin
7. Jumpa
8. Whatzit
9. Storm
10. Topo
11. Ark
12. Hoppy
13. Batcow
14. Big Ted
15. Proty
16. Gleek
17. Paw Pooch
18. Bull Dog
19. Chameleon Collie
20. Hot Dog
21. Tail Terrier
22. Tusky Husky
23. Mammoth Mutt
24. Dawg
25. B'dg
26. Stripezoid
27. Zallion
28. Ribitz
29. Bzzd
30. Gratch
31. Buzzoo
32. Fossfur
33. Zhoomp
34. Eeny

 1
 2
 3
 4

 5
 6
 7
 8

 9
 10
 11
 12

 13
 14
 15
 16

 17
 18
 19
 20

 21
 22
 23
 24

 25
 26
 27
 28

 29
30
31
 32
 33
 34

KNOW YOUR VILLAIN PETS

1. Bizarro Krypto
2. Ignatius
3. Rozz
4. Mechanikat
5. Crackers
6. Giggles
7. Joker Fish
8. Chauncey
9. Artie Puffin
10. Griff
11. Waddles
12. Dogwood
13. Mr. Mind
14. Sobek
15. Misty
16. Sneezers
17. General Manx
18. Nizz
19. Fer-El
20. Titano
21. Bit-Bit
22. X-43
23. Dex-Starr
24. Glomulus
25. Whoosh
26. Pronto
27. Snorrt
28. Rolf
29. Tootz
30. Eezix
31. Donald
32. Waxxee
33. Fimble
34. Webbik

 1
 2
 3
 4

 5
 6
 7
 8

 9
 10
 11
 12

 13
 14
 15
 16

 17
 18
 19
 *20*

 21
 22
 23
 *24*

 25
 26
 27
 28

 29
 30
 31
 32
 33
 34

JOKES

What do you call a fly with no wings?

No idea.

A walk!

What do you call spiders that just got married?

Tell me.

Newly-webs!

Why was the mother firefly happy?

Tell me.

Because her children were all so bright!

GLOSSARY

antennae feelers on the head of an insect

corps group acting together or doing the same thing

dugout shelter where baseball players sit when they are not batting or in the field

grand slam home run hit when all the bases are occupied by players. A grand slam scores four runs, which is the highest possible.

home plate where the batter stands and over which the pitcher must throw the ball. To score a run, the batter must touch the home plate after having reached all the other bases.

oath formal promise

reinforcements additional members of a group that strengthen its power

universe planets, stars, and all things that exist in space

MEET THE AUTHOR

Jane B. Mason

Jane B. Mason is no super hero, but having three kids sometimes makes her wish she had superpowers. Jane has written children's books for more than fifteen years and hopes to continue doing so for fifty more. She lives with her husband, three children, their dog, and a gecko.

MEET THE ILLUSTRATOR

Eisner Award-winner Art Baltazar

Art Baltazar defines cartoons and comics not only as a style of art, but as a way of life. Art is the creative force behind *The New York Times* best-selling, Eisner Award-winning, DC Comics series Tiny Titans, and the co-writer for *Billy Batson and the Magic of SHAZAM!* Art draws comics and never has to leave the house. He lives with his lovely wife, Rose, big boy Sonny, little boy Gordon, and little girl Audrey.

ART BALTAZAR says:

Read all the DC SUPER-PETS stories today!

Raintree is an imprint of Capstone Global Library Limited, a company
incorporated in England and Wales having its registered office at 264 Banbury
Road, Oxford, OX2 7DY – Registered company number: 6695582

www.raintree.co.uk
myorders@raintree.co.uk

First published by Picture Window Books in 2012
First published in the United Kingdom in 2012
The moral rights of the proprietor have been asserted.

Art Director and Designer: Bob Lentz
Editors: Donald Lemke and Vaarunika Dharmapala
Creative Director: Heather Kindseth
Editorial Director: Michael Dahl

ISBN 978 1 4747 6447 6 (paperback)
21 20 19 18 17
10 9 8 7 6 5 4 3 2 1

British Library Cataloguing in Publication Data
A full catalogue record for this book is available from the British Library.

Printed and bound in India